Superphonics **Storybooks will help your child to learn to read using Ruth Misk**  **phonic method. Each story is** ... **been carefully written to incl** ... **and spellings.**

The Storybooks are graded so your child can progress with confidence from easy words to harder ones. There are four levels - Blue (the easiest), Green, Purple and Turquoise (the hardest). Each level is linked to one of the core *Superphonics*® Books.

ISBN: 978 0 340 79895 9

Text copyright © 2001 Gill Munton
Illustrations copyright © 2001 Mike Gibbie

Editorial by Gill Munton
Design by Sarah Borny

The rights of Gill Munton and Mike Gibbie to be identified as the author and illustrator of this Work have been asserted by them in accordance with the Copyright, Designs and Patents Act 1988.

First published in Great Britain 2001

10 9 8 7 6 5 4 3

First published in 2001 by Hodder Children's Books,
a division of Hachette Children's Books,
338 Euston Road, London NW1 3BH
An Hachette UK Company. www.hachette.co.uk

Printed and bound in China by WKT Company Ltd.

A CIP record is registered by and held at the British Library.

Target words

This Purple Storybook focuses on the following sounds:

ow as in **grow** | **oa** as in **boat**
o-e as in **hole**

These target words are featured in the book:

below	shallow	rope	groan
blow	show	rose	groaned
bowl	slow	tones	groans
flows	slowly		moaned
grow	towed	afloat	oats
know	willow	boat	road
low	yellow	boats	soap
meadow		coat	soaped
narrow	hole	float	stoat
own	home	floating	throat
rowing	hope	goat	toad
			toads

(Words containing sounds and spellings practised in the Blue and Green Storybooks and the other Purple Storybooks have been used in the story, too.)

Other words

Also included are some common words (e.g. **have**, **the**) which your child will be learning in his or her first few years at school.

A few other words have been used to help the story to flow.

Reading the book

1 Make sure you and your child are sitting in a quiet, comfortable place.

2 Tell him or her a little about the story, without giving too much away:

This is the story of a goat in a boat - who wants to go home. His friends, Sister Stoat and Brother Toad, come to his rescue.

This will give your child a mental picture; having a context for a story makes it easier to read the words.

3 Read the target words (above) together. This will mean that you can both enjoy the story without having to spend too much time working out the words. Help your child to sound out each word (e.g. **g-oa-t**) before saying the whole word.

4 Let your child read the story aloud. Help him or her with any difficult words and discuss the story as you go along. Stop now and again to ask your child to predict what will happen next. This will help you to see whether he or she has understood what has happened so far.

Above all, enjoy the story, and praise your child's reading!

Ruth Miskin's
Superphonics®
Purple Storybook

A Goat
in a Boat

by Gill Munton

Illustrated by Mike Gibbie

Hodder
Children's
Books

a division of Hachette Children's Books

In a place I know, a willow tree grows,

And below that tree, a river flows.

And on that river, all afloat,

Was a red and yellow rowing boat.

Dozy Duck had a look inside,

There was lots of room

for someone to hide!

"Dangling duckweed, it's a goat –

A big, black goat, afloat in a boat!"

A big, black goat with big black feet,

As big a goat as you could meet!

The goat looked at Dozy;
  she said to the goat:

"Why are you floating about
  in that boat?"

The goat gave a groan,

   and he looked very sad.

"Well, life in a boat's not SO very bad –

But it's hard to keep clean,

   and it's hard to keep warm

When the boat sails into

   a very bad storm.

Will you get me a bowl of shaving cream,
And some soap, so I can wash in a stream?

Will you get me a nice warm winter coat?
That's what a goat needs for a life afloat!"

So Dozy said goodbye to the goat,

And went to get her winter coat,

And her very own cake of

   rose petal soap:

"This will please the goat, I hope!"

The goat soaped his beard

  (he was still in the boat),

And did the coat up at his throat.

And then he said, in tones soft and low:

"I want to go back to where

  green grasses grow!"

So Dozy called to Sister Stoat.

They put a rope about the goat's throat.

And then came the groans of
the goat in the boat:

"To the bank of the river I'll slowly float!"

So the stoat towed the goat

(afloat in the boat)

With his shiny clean beard

and his new winter coat,

To the shallow water by the bank.

The goat got out –

and the rowing boat sank!

"I'm glad I've seen the last of that boat!"

Moaned the goat in the coat

  (no longer afloat),

And then he said, in tones soft and low:

"I want to go back to where

green grasses grow!"

"Well, don't look at me!" said Sister Stoat.

"It's tired me out, keeping you afloat.

I'm going home now, to a bowl

of hot oats.

My advice to you is:

Stay away from all boats!"

The goat looked at Dozy;
she looked at the goat.

"I know who will help a goat in a coat –
He lives on his own, in a hole
in the road –
I'll show you where to find Brother Toad!"

So Dozy Duck and the goat in the coat

Trotted away from the sinking boat.

And when they came to the
  hole in the road
A face popped up – it was Brother Toad!

"Brother Toad, meet the goat in the coat!
(He used to be called the goat
  in the boat).

And this, my dear goat, is Brother Toad!
(This is where he lives –
  in this hole in the road.)"

And then the goat said,
  in tones soft and low:
"I want to go back to where
  green grasses go!
Please will you take me, Brother Toad?
(If you don't mind leaving your hole
  in the road.)"

The goat in the new winter coat

  and the toad

Went off down the narrow yellow road.

The road was hard,

  and the road was slow,

(But toads always know the way to go.)

And after their journey, long and hard,

They came to a farm, and went

   into the yard,

And into a meadow

   (where green grasses grow,

And bend, and shake,

   as the soft winds blow).

But the goat groaned:

"I don't think I like what I see –

It's funny how dull a meadow can be.

A meadow is really no place for a goat.

I think I would like –

   to be back in my boat!"